THIS WALKER BOOK BELONGS TO:

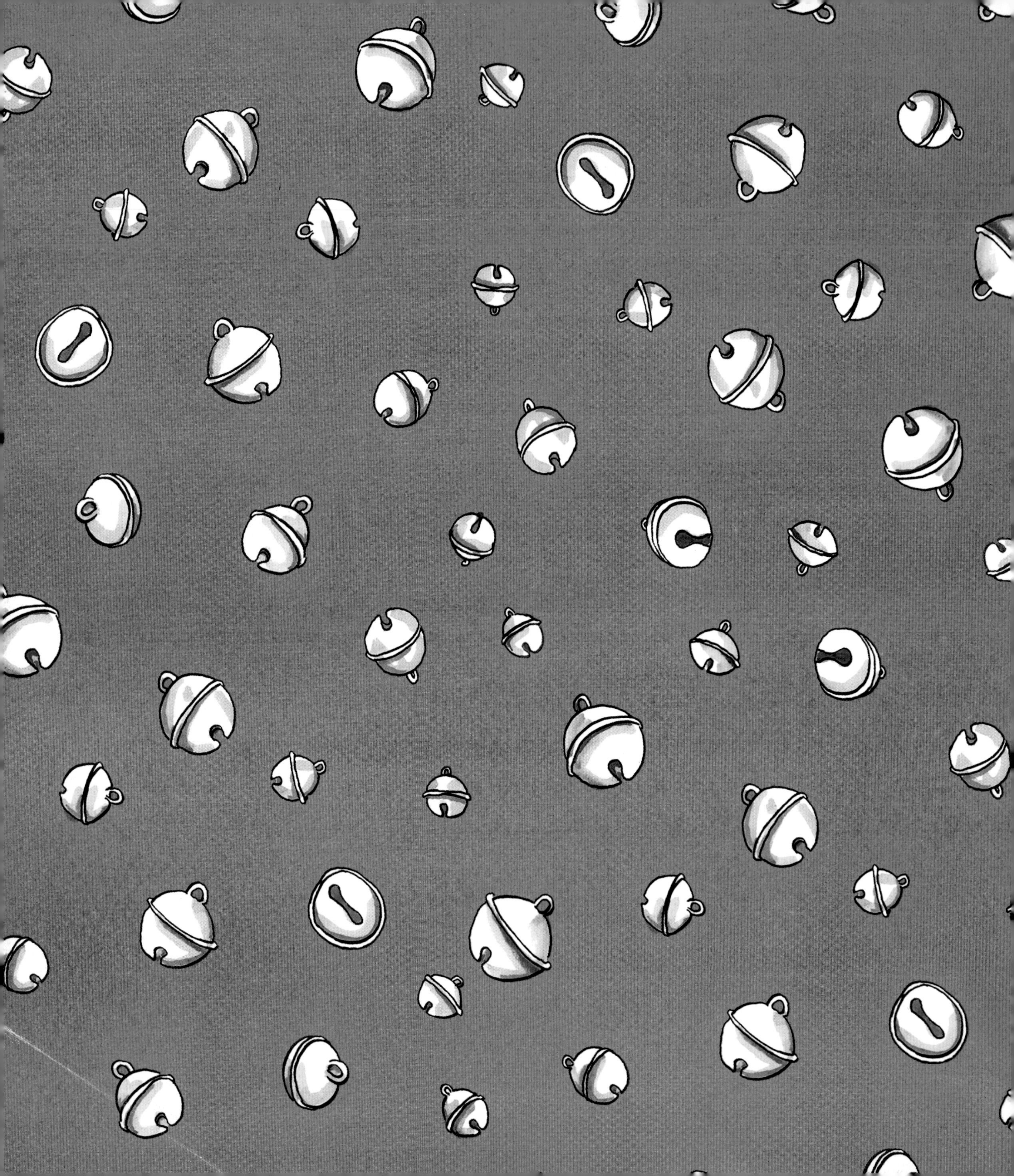

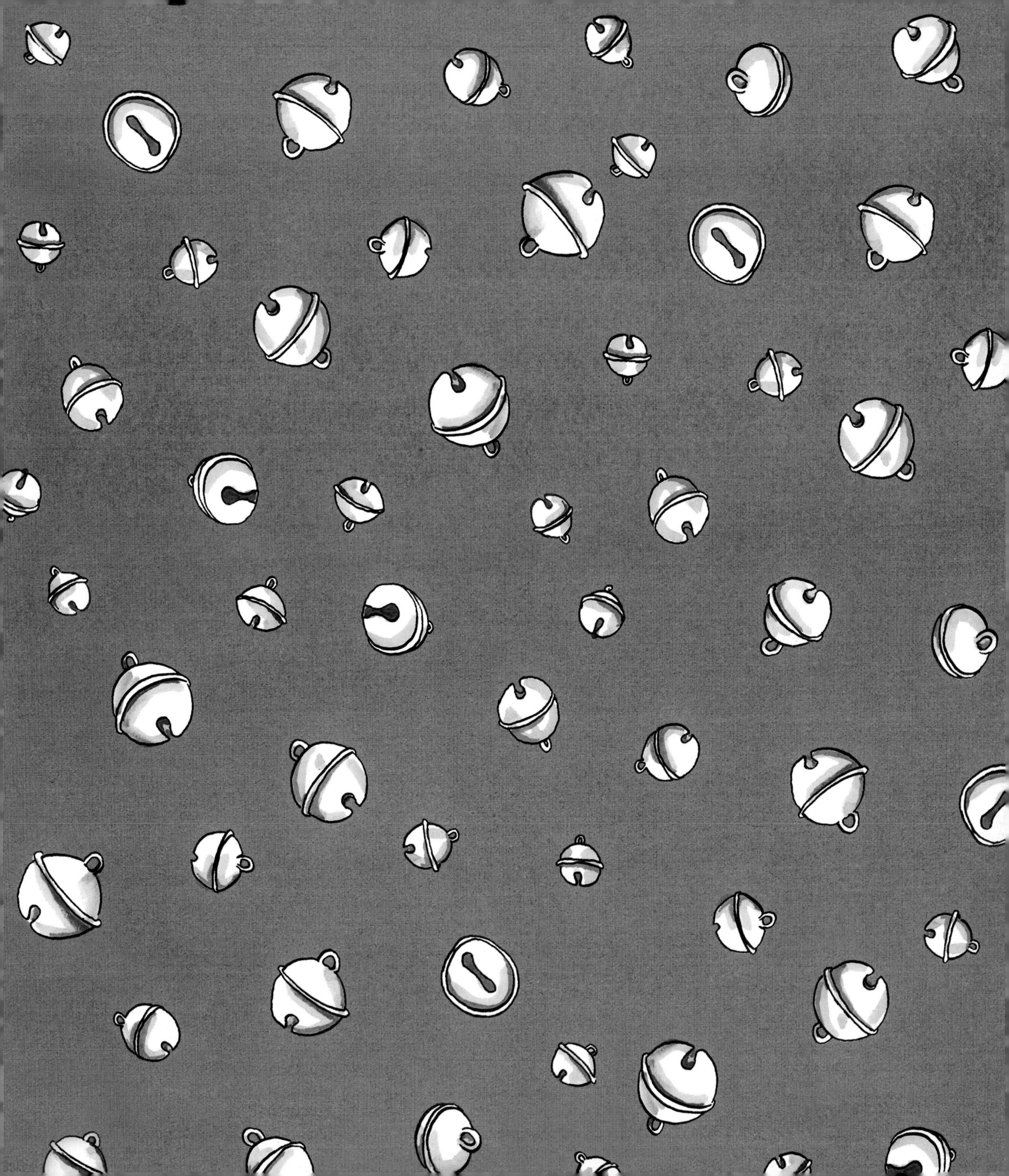

For Fergus

First published 1995 by Walker Books Ltd
87 Vauxhall Walk, London SE11 5HJ

This edition published 2004

10 9 8 7 6 5 4 3 2 1

The book has been typeset in Columbus

Printed in China

British Library Cataloguing in Publication Data:
a catalogue record for this book is available from the British Library

ISBN 1-84428-459-X

www.walkerbooks.co.uk

Daisy Dare

Anita Jeram

WALKER BOOKS
AND SUBSIDIARIES
LONDON • BOSTON • SYDNEY • AUCKLAND

Daisy Dare did things
her friends were far
too scared to do.
"Just dare me," she said.
"Anything you like.
I'm never,
ever scared!"

So they dared her to walk
the garden wall.

They dared her to eat a worm.

They dared her to
stick out her tongue
at Miss Crumb.
And she did!

One day,
Daisy's friends
thought of
a really scary
dare to do.

They whispered it to Daisy.
“I’m not doing that!” she said.
“Daisy Dare-not!” they laughed.

Daisy took
a deep breath.
"All right," she said.
"I'll do it."
This was the dare:
to take the bell off
the cat's collar.

The cat
was asleep.
That
was good.

The bell
slipped off
easily.
That was
good too.

But Daisy's hands
trembled so much
that the bell tinkled,
the cat woke up ...

and that was

very,

very

bad!

Daisy ran
and ran
as fast as she could,
back to
her friends,
through
the garden gate,
and into the house

where the
cat couldn't
follow.

"Phew!" said Billy.
"Wow!" gasped Joe.
"You're the bravest,
most daring mouse in the whole
world!" shouted Contrary Mary.
Daisy Dare grinned with pride.
"Just dare me," she said.
"Anything you like...

I'm only *sometimes* scared!"

Little Baa
Kim Lewis
GUESS HOW MUCH I LOVE YOU
Sam McBratney
Anita Jeram
MAX
BOB GRAHAM
We're Going on a Bear Hunt
Michael Rosen
Helen Oxenbury
OWL BABIES
GORILLA
Maisy's Bedtime
Lucy Cousins
Leon and Bob
Simon James
The Large Family
Five Minutes' Peace
JILL MURPHY
HUG
JEZ ALBOROUGH

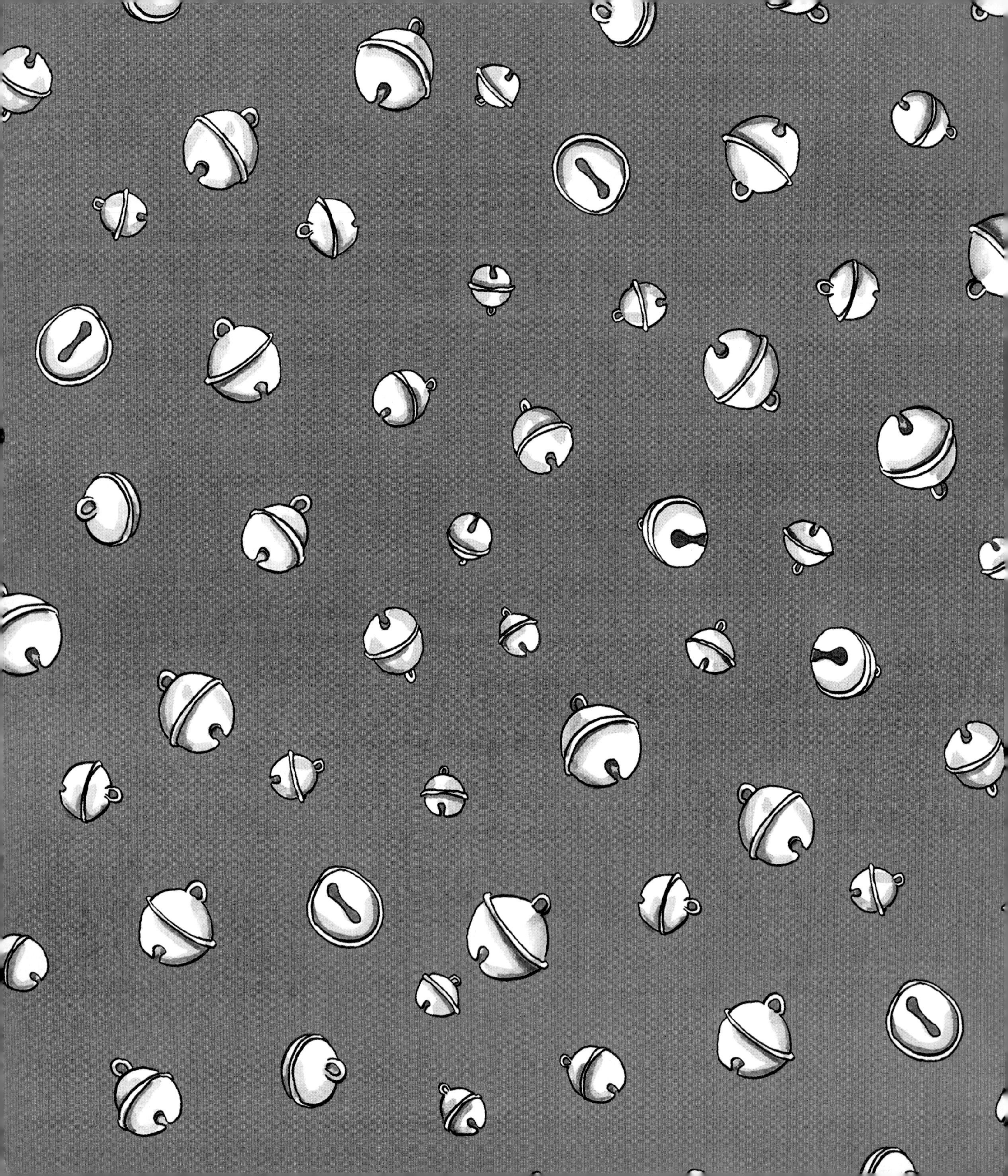

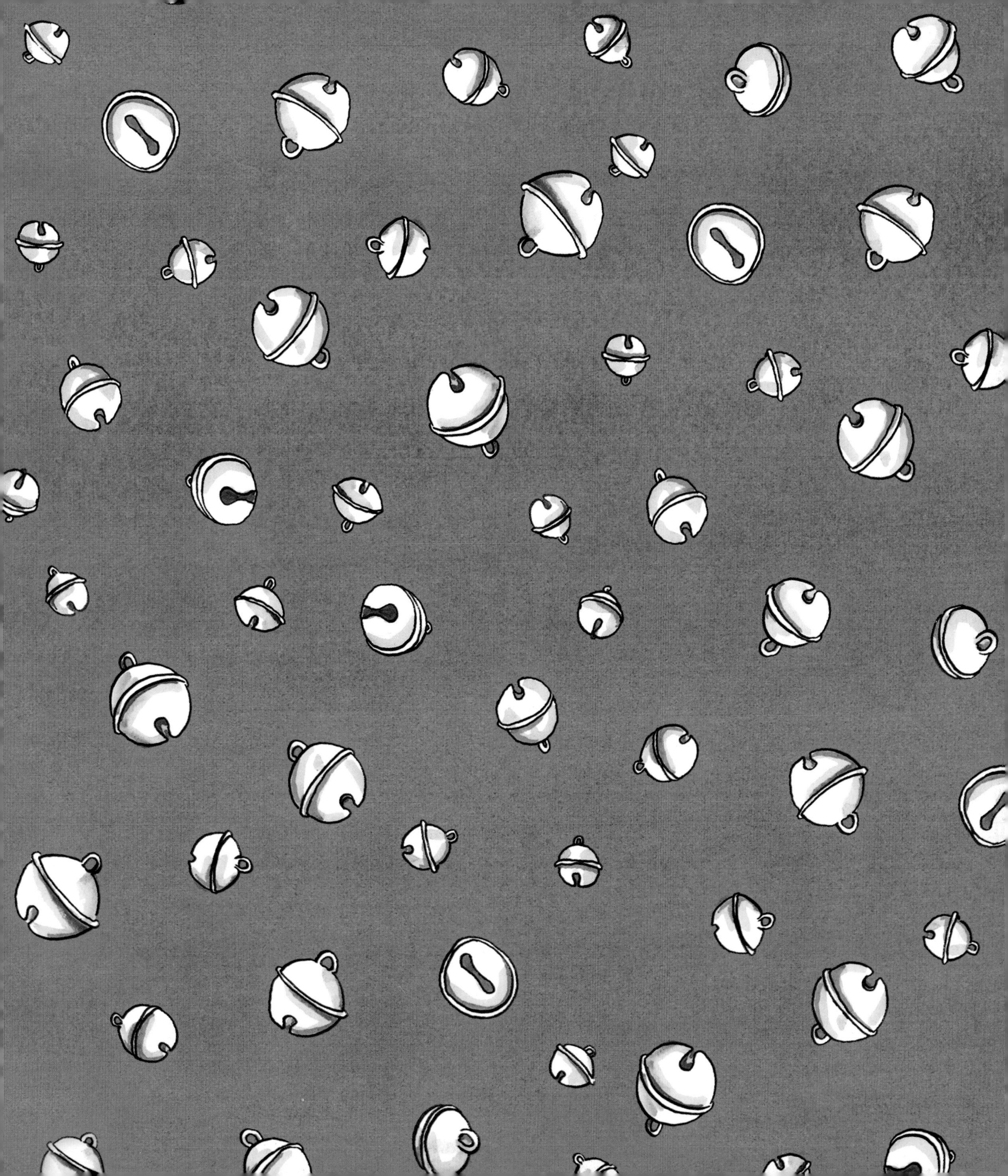